MW01047194

A Tale of Horned Owls

By Yasmin John-Thorpe   Photos from the Residents of Quail Creek

This book grew out of the keen interest of the residents whose imagination was piqued at the birth of owlets in a palm tree at Quail Creek, AZ. Thank you to everyone who gave me permission to use their photographs of the event as it unfolded in the early spring of 2019:

My sincere appreciation to editor Norma Hill, typesetter Dawn Renaud and proofreader Barbara Gordon. Yasmin's back cover photo courtesy of Stuart Bish Photography.

My thanks also to Stephanie Salsnek for the use of her late husband's painting of horned owls on the cover of this book. *I hereby authorize Yasmin John-Thorpe to use the image of "Hooters" by John Salsnek for the exclusive purpose of the cover of her book. This image will become public domain December 31, 2067. No other publication may use this image and it may not be copied or reproduced for any other purpose not related to Ms. John-Thorpe's publication. Stephanie Alm Salsnek, Executrix and Gallery Manager for The Art & Legacy of John Salsnek*

This book is the creation of the author Yasmin John-Thorpe. Copyright 2019, Yasmin John-Thorpe, British Columbia, Canada. All rights reserved.

All photos are the property of the photographers.
ISBN: 9781080787852
Printed and bound in the United States of America

Other books in this series, for readers to 8 years:
> *A Home for the Q's*
> *Cruz Coyote & Rory Roadrunner*
> *The Adventures of Cruz Coyote*
> *Cruz and the Pack*
> *The Adventures of Hummer Hummingbird*
> *Jenry, the Silly Javelina*

Coming Soon
> *What Am I? ABC's from the Sonoran Desert Books*

Suitable for babies:
> *Goodnight, Sonoran Friends*

Other books, for readers 8 to 14 years:
Grandpa's Gift - recounting the Canadians' WWI Battle to win Vimy Ridge
Two Unlikely Heroes of the New World - an adventure story of a young Spaniard and his Mayan friend
Just Nuts - a book about various kinds of nuts and nut allergies

Romance books for adults
Forever - Josh & Petra
Always - Marissa & Tyler
Bewitched - Maggie & Howard

Yasmin John-Thorpe's books are available from Amazon under the author's name.

In Memory of

John Salsnek
1947 - 2017
Paw Prints Studio & Gallery: The Legacy & Art of John Salsnek
Nature Artist, Philanthropist, Illustrator, Pet Dad Extraordinaire

Olin E. Gordon
1943 - 2018
US Air Force 1961 - 1988
Dept. of Veterans Affairs 1994 - 2007

Izabelle Megan Xi Shi Preddie
my grandniece
who first asked for an owl story after seeing photos.

Cover image: John Salsnek
Photo credits for each page (clockwise from top left):

1 Yasmin John-Thorpe

2-3 Rick Thorpe

3 Jeff Krueger

4-5 Jeff Krueger

5 Janice Swain, Jeff Krueger

6 Lauren Hillquist

7 Lauren Hillquist,
D.L. Mutter

8 Jeff Krueger,
Lauren Hillquist

9 Jeff Krueger

10 Lauren Hillquist (both)

11 Marcia Sutton,
Lauren Hillquist

12 Cheryl Anthony,
Lauren Hillquist (twice)

13 Linda Roeller (both)

14 Diane Nickolas (including
close-up)

15 Jeff Krueger

16 Lauren Hillquist,
Janice Swain

17 Janice Swain,
Yasmin John-Thorpe

18 Images by Ables

19 Ann Nease

20-21 Walt Obremski

21 Jeff Krueger,
Images by Ables

22 Marcia Sutton

23 Images by Ables (both)

24 Jeff Krueger

25 Edna Barisoff,
Yasmin John-Thorpe,
Kathi Krieg,
Bobbi Gordon

26 Lauren Hillquist,
Yasmin John-Thorpe

27 Yasmin John-Thorpe (both)

28 Jeff Krueger (both)

29 Images by Ables

30 Yasmin John-Thorpe,
Images by Ables

32 Yasmin John-Thorpe

About the Characters

Odin and Ossana Owl are great horned owls. The male has a larger voice box so his hoots are deeper than the female. The female is larger in size than the male. She will lay eggs early in the year, sometimes as early as February. They sometimes do not build their own nests; instead they use old raven and hawk nests to raise their young.

Owls are powerful predators and can only lift their own body weight (around 2 to 3 pounds). When they close their talons around a prey it takes about 28 pounds of force to open them. They capture a very wide range of prey, including reptiles, amphibians, rodents, and birds.

Great horned owls see better in the dark as they have large eyes, with pupils that open wide in darkness giving them excellent night vision. They can turn their head 180 degrees and have great hearing. Great horned owls can live long lives, maybe up to 28 years.

Bryce Bobcat is a desert bobcat. Adult bobcats weigh between 15 and 35 pounds and can be up to three feet long. Their colors range from gray-brown to reddish brown. Some can be steel blue with dark spots on their fur for camouflage. Their main competitor for food is the coyote.

Cruz Coyote is a desert coyote. These are a smaller coyote with a lighter-tinted coat. They are naturally curious animals that roam the hot Sonoran Desert hunting small rodents. Coyotes live in packs with other coyotes.

Jaxon and Jen Jackrabbit are antelope jackrabbits. A jackrabbit's long ears help regulate its body temperature. The ears stand erect in hot weather to give off heat, which cools the body. They lay back in cool weather to constrict blood flow to keep the body warm.

Hudson Hawk is red-tail hawk. Only the adults have the distinctive red feathers on their tails. They nest in spring, sometimes constructing their platform nest on a saguaro cactus. They hunt rodents, rabbits, squirrels, birds and snakes. They hunt in pairs, perched on a tree, or soar up to check their territory. Females lay one to five eggs, and both parents take turns sitting on the eggs to keep them safe and warm.

Winter comes to the Sonoran Desert. In the community of Quail Creek the days are sunny but cool, and snow falls on the distant mountain tops. However, this New Year's morning is different. The residents wake up to a surprise.

The sun disappears behind clouds. A white blanket of snow covers the cacti, the trees, even the fruits. The ground becomes a cold, white fluffy blanket. The wintry weather even turns the waterfalls into ice.

The snow falls again in early February. The unusual weather confuses many Sonoran Desert dwellers who witness this sudden change to their normal daily routine.

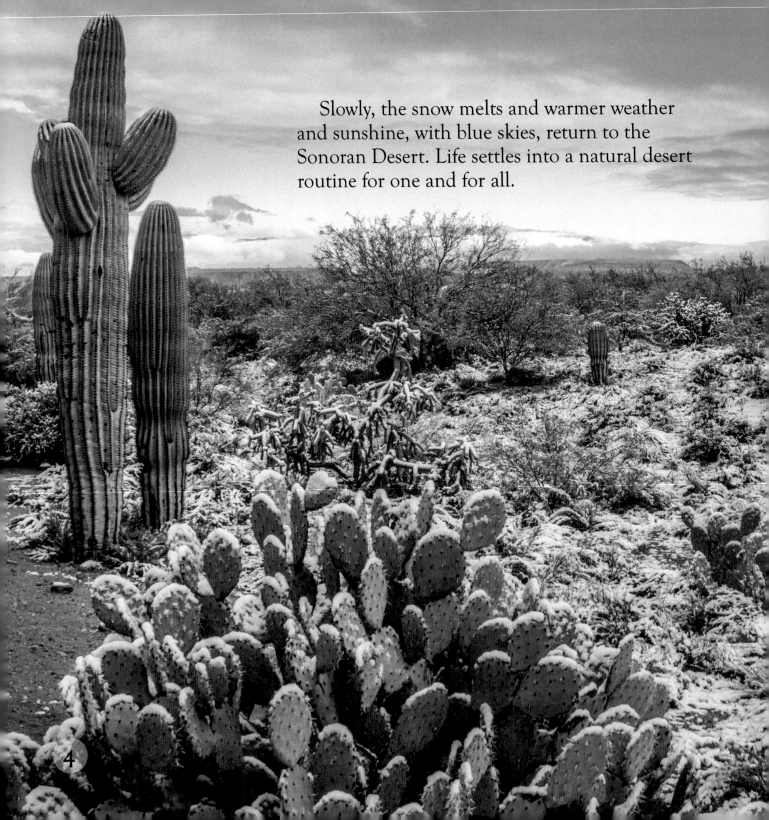

Slowly, the snow melts and warmer weather and sunshine, with blue skies, return to the Sonoran Desert. Life settles into a natural desert routine for one and for all.

It is early spring and it is the season for Odin Owl and his mate, Ossana to start a family. Odin looks around and suggests a nest in a nearby tall palm tree. Ossana has used the nest before so she checks it out again.

5

Ossana Owl agrees and snuggles into the frond. She patiently waits for her eggs. It is very windy and the palm tree sways. Soon Ossana lays four eggs in the frond nest and Odin is a proud daddy.

It takes almost thirty-four days before a little girl owlet, Odette, hatches. Ossana keeps the other eggs warm as the days are cool. Soon there is a little boy owlet, Otis, then another girl owlet, Oakie, pops out of her egg. Finally, another boy, Olin, is hatched.

The nest is overcrowded with four babies. The spring winds pick up and the palm tree sways. When a gust blows hard, Odette falls out of the nest to the ground below. She is scared. Wildlife is called and arrives to take owlet Odette away to feed her and keep her safe.

8

Ossana keeps watch over her other babies. The owlets are growing and this creates a problem in keeping them protected in the nest. Ossana and Odin must also take turns hunting to feed the owlets.

9

Oakie is curious and peeks beyond her mom to check all that is happening around the nest. One day, as Ossana watches from high in the palm tree, Oakie loses her balance and slips out of the nest. Luckily, she lands on another palm frond below the nest.

Oakie remains where she lands. She is scared and checks below. Oakie is still very high up and now has to wait for her parents to bring her food.

She misses her brothers, Otis and Olin.

Still in the nest with their mom Ossana are two owlets. She watches over them as they grow. But Ossana worries as it is not safe for any of the owlets.

When the winds get strong and the palm sways, Otis falls out of the high perch and lands on the ground. He is frightened. Hopping behind a nearby wall so he is out of the way, Otis searches for somewhere safe.

13

With help, Otis is carefully placed in a crate, high off the ground in a nearby tree for his safety away from predators. The crate is covered with dried palm fronds leaving room for Ossana and Odin to feed Otis. Odette survives and is brought back and also placed in the crate.

Odette and Otis constantly get out of the crate and venture around.

Oakie remains alone on the frond.

Olin is the only owlet still high up in the nest with his mom. He is growing bigger every day but he is lonely.

Ossana and Odin continue to hunt at night bringing food to all the owlets. Ossana worries about the dangerous predators who might harm one or all of her owlets. She has seen Hudson Hawk in a nearby tree.

She knows Bryce Bobcat also hunts in the area.

And, Cruz Coyote has been seen roaming close, hunting for his next meal.

17

Happy to see her owlets learning to be on their own, Ossana stands high up in a palm tree to watch her eldest owlet Odette as she leaves the crate and finds safety in a nearby tree.

Once there, Odette
keeps watch all around.

Soon Otis and Oakie make it to the mesquite tree. They are close to Odette. The owlets continue to spread their wings, moving away from the nest area. They are still being fed by their mom and dad.

Odette moves away from her brothers to another tree to stand alone. Otis now keeps watch over Oakie, who is still very small. Otis shelters Oakie to keeps her warm on windy, cool nights.

23

Odette remains away from her brothers on a nearby tree and stands alone. She is getting bigger and her wings are growing. She stays alert and curious, checking all around as she keeps watch.

24

Spring arrives in the Sonoran Desert. Cacti and wild flowers show off their beautiful blooms. The ocotillo proudly display their red candles. Nearby pecan trees burst into green leaves.

Away from his siblings, Olin is alone in the nest. He becomes strong enough to leave the nest and hops down to a nearby tree where he waits for food from his parents.

While the owlets grow, the palo verde trees show off yellow blossoms as the birds sing loudly and doves coo. Jackson Jackrabbit and his mate Jen come out of their home under the ground to play and to search for food.

27

The four owlets continue to grow bigger. Ossana and Odin continue to bring food to feed the owlets.

One day Odette, the eldest, is the first to leave her perch and fly away.

Then Otis leaves Oakie all alone.

Even Olin leaves
his perch and flies off.

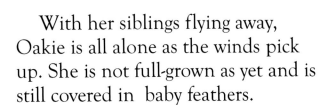

With her siblings flying away, Oakie is all alone as the winds pick up. She is not full-grown as yet and is still covered in baby feathers.

Oakie must cling to the branch with her talons to keep from losing her balance.

Several days later, Oakie too is gone. The owlets have flown off one by one to be safely with their parents.

Ossana and Odin must now teach the owlets how to hunt for their food.

Fragrant blossoms fill the air as the
Sonoran Desert moves into warmer
weather.
All is well with the horned owls.

A Tale of Horned Owls

COMPREHENSION EXERCISE

Readers, test your knowledge:

1. What type of owls are in this story?

2. Name the mom and dad owls.

3. How many eggs does the mom have?

4. Which owl is hatched first?

5. Can you name the owlets? How many boys? How many girls?

6. Who is the tiniest owlet?

7. Which owlet falls out of the nest first?

8. What predators are hanging around?

9. Who is being a big brother?

10. Which owlets fly away first, second, and third, and who is the last one to leave?

ISBN 978-1540382702 (U.S.A.)
ISBN 978-0-9921245-2-6 (Canada)

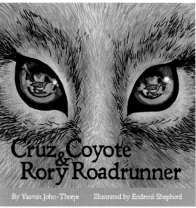

ISBN 978-1540382979 (U.S.A.)
ISBN 978-0-9921245-4-0 (Canada)

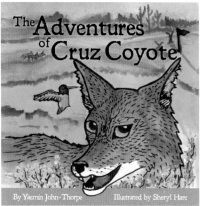

ISBN 978-1518795855 (U.S.A.)
ISBN 978-0-9921245-6-4 (Canada)

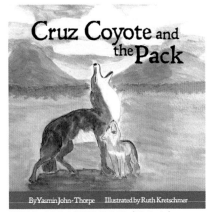

ISBN: 978-1537462042 (U.S.A.)
ISBN: 978-0-9921245-7-1 (Canada)

ISBN: 978-1977535771 (U.S.A.)
ISBN: 978-0-9959843-1-8 (Canada)

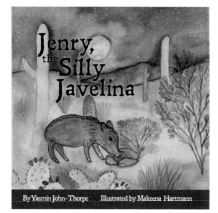

ISBN: 978-1726493581 (U.S.A.)

ISBN: 978-1976577956 (U.S.A.)
ISBN: 978-0-9959843-2-5 (Canada)

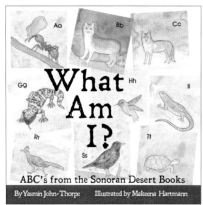

ISBN: 9781692812843 (U.S.A.)

ISBN: 9781080787852 (U.S.A.)